Seasonal Adventures

by Johnny Ray Moore

illustrated by Cbabi Bayoc

To my handsome grandson, Ethan O'Bryan Young;
my darling granddaughter, Jade Olivia Young;
and all children, near and far —J.R.M.

This is dedicated to my three children, and I hope they
know I will be by their side through every season
they experience. —Cbabi Bayoc

Welcome to Spring!

Tireless tadpoles
Swim with ease.

North Wind gently
Combs the trees.

Green grass growing
On a hill
Newborn, chirping
Whippoorwills.

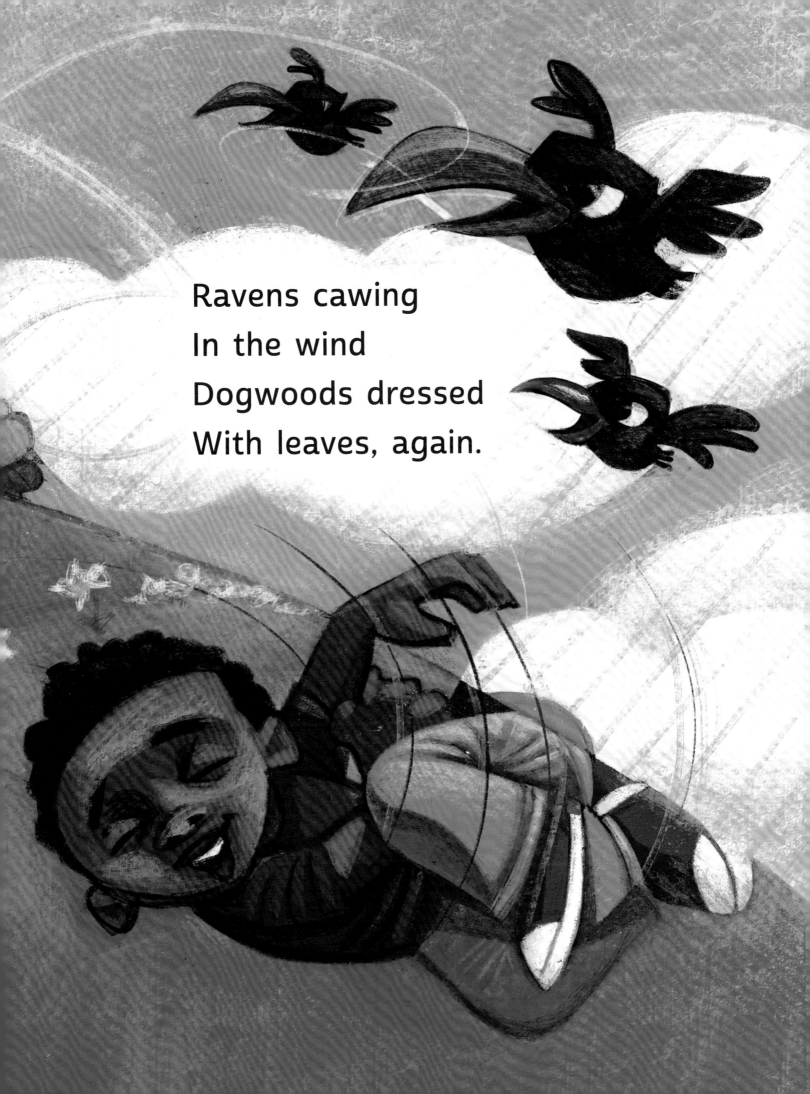

Ravens cawing
In the wind
Dogwoods dressed
With leaves, again.

Quails astir
About the field
Amongst the shrubs
Are daffodils.

April showers
Somewhat soon
Cloudless skies, again,
By noon.

Life's anew
With sounds unheard
All because
Spring has occurred.

Welcome to

Summer!

Sunrays dancing

Ponies prancing

Kittens on their mother's back.

Frogs all **hoppy**

Puddles **sloppy**

Ducks are going

QUACK!
QUACK!
QUACK!

Thunder crashing
Lightning flashing
Raindrops cooling thirsty Earth.

People cheering
Dusk appearing
Runners racing
To be first.

Daisies blooming
Cats assuming
Dogs are sleeping
On the lawn.

Daylight fading
Cows parading
Back to shelter
At the barn.

Welcome to
SUMMER!

Welcome to
Fall!

Mornings with
A bit of chill
Jack Frost sprinkled
Down the hill.

Stacks of hay
All turning brown
Lined so neatly
On the ground.

Farmers plowing
Fields now bare
Leaves all scattered
Here and there.

Acorns from
The mighty oak
Chimneys coughing
Puffs of smoke.

Supper at
The brink of dusk
Plates all filled
With just enough.

Twinkling stars
At evening's end
Let us know
Fall now begins.

Welcome to FALL!

Mice are searching
In the earth
Lone wolf howls
For all it's worth.

Furry bunnies
Near a cave
Watching chipmunks
Misbehave.

Reindeer nosy
With their stares
Snoring, fuzzy
Wuzzy bears.

Leaves of color
Scattered 'round
Covering tracks
Upon the ground.

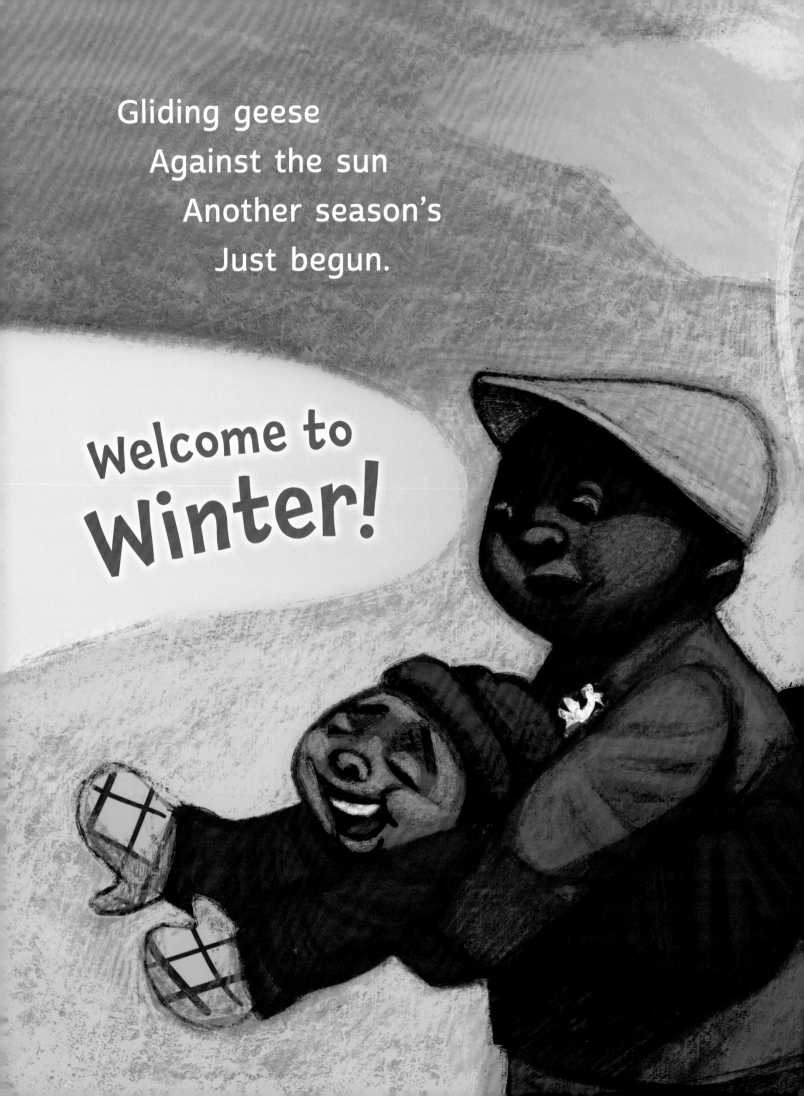

Gliding geese
Against the sun
Another season's
Just begun.

Welcome to
Winter!

MEET
Johnny Ray Moore

Johnny Ray Moore is a poet, children's book author, greeting cards writer, and songwriter. He wrote his first poem when he was in the third grade. Johnny is a graduate of the Institute of Children's Literature and a member of the Society of Children's Book Writers and Illustrators. He lives in Knightdale, North Carolina, with his wife and one of their three daughters.

MEET Cbabi Bayoc

Cbabi (pronounced *Kuh-bob-bi*) Bayoc is an artist living in St. Louis, Missouri. His work has been described as unique, bold, and colorful, while adding some "phunk." Bayoc, whose given name is Clifford Miskell, Jr., adopted his name CBABI (Creative-Black-Artist-Battling-Ignorance) during his time at Grambling State University. BAYOC (Blessed-African-Youth-Of-Creativity) provided a unique and deep connection that would one day be shared with his children. Cbabi has created artwork for Prince, Muhammad Ali, and *Rap Pages* magazine, and his murals can be seen all over St. Louis. He is well known for his *365 Days with Dad* series, which paints a positive image of Black fatherhood.